CUPCAKES

APPLES

CHEESE

MUSHROOMS

FISH

MUD

ROCKS

BROCCOLI

PEPPERONI

SMELLY SOCK

BLUEBERRIES

ONIONS

To my pizza lovers—you have a PIZZA my heart!
Proverbs 17:17
—K.D.

Ephesians 4:32
—J.D.

Pete the Cat and the Perfect Pizza Party
Text copyright © 2019 by Kimberly and James Dean
Illustrations copyright © 2019 by James Dean
Pete the Cat is a registered trademark of Pete the Cat, LLC.
All rights reserved. Manufactured in China.
No part of this book may be used or reproduced in any manner whatsoever without
written permission except in the case of brief quotations embodied in critical articles and reviews.
For information address HarperCollins Children's Books, a division of HarperCollins Publishers,
195 Broadway, New York, NY 10007.
www.harpercollinschildrens.com
Library of Congress Control Number: 2018962096
ISBN 978-0-06-240437-4 (trade bdg.)
ISBN 978-0-06-240910-2 (lib. bdg.)
The artist used pen and ink with watercolor and acrylic paint on
300lb press paper to create the illustrations for this book.
Typography by Jeanne L. Hogle
19 20 21 22 23   SCP   10 9 8 7 6 5 4 3 2 1
❖
First Edition

Pete the Cat

and the
Perfect Pizza Party

Kimberly and
James Dean

HARPER

An Imprint of HarperCollins*Publishers*

Pete the Cat LOVES pizza!
Pete the Cat LOVES parties TOO!
Pete had an idea of what he could DO!

He would have the **PERFECT**

PIZZA PARTY!

Pete's friends all arrived.

It was time to build the **PERFECT PIZZA** together.

That would make the pizza even better!

Pete thought the perfect pizza would be pepperoni with extra cheese!

But everyone did not agree!

Callie said, "Pepperoni would be just fine.
But I really love PRETZELS on mine."

Pete and the gang were puzzled.

"PRETZELS?"

Well, *that's* something new.
But maybe PRETZELS could be groovy too!

Squirrel said, "Pepperoni and pretzels would be just fine. But I really love pistachios on mine!"

Pete and the gang were puzzled.

"PISTACHIOS?"

Well, *that's* something new.
But maybe PISTACHIOS could be groovy too!

Grumpy Toad said, "Pepperoni, pretzels, and pistachios would be just fine. But I really love pickles on mine!"

Pete and the gang were puzzled.

"PICKLES?"

Well, *that's* something new.
But maybe PICKLES could be groovy too!

"It's a party,
a party,
a PEPPERONI PRETZEL PISTACHIO Pi

Gus said, "Pepperoni, pretzels, pistachios, and pickles would be just fine. But I really love popcorn on mine!"

Pete and the gang were puzzled.

"POPCORN?"

Well, *that's* something new.
But maybe POPCORN could be groovy too!

"It's a party,
a party,
a PEPPERONI PRETZEL PISTACHIO

PICKLE POPCORN
pizza party!"

Alligator said, "Pepperoni, pretzels, pistachios, pickles, and popcorn would be just fine. But I really love papaya on mine!"

Now Pete and the gang were really puzzled.

"PAPAYA?"

Well, *that's* something new.
But maybe PAPAYA could be groovy too!

"It's a party,
a party,
a PEPPERONI PRETZEL
PISTACHIO PICKLE
POPCORN PAPAYA
pizza party!"

Pete and the gang piled the PEPPERONI, PRETZELS, PISTACHIOS, PICKLES, POPCORN, and PAPAYA on top.

The PIZZA was so high they had to STOP!

DING! The pizza was done!

Trying something new might be FUN!
They all built up the courage to take a first **BITE!**

And the PEPPERONI PRETZEL PISTACHIO PICKLE
POPCORN PAPAYA PIZZA was . . .

OUT OF SIGHT!!!!!.... (DYNAMITE, JUST RIGHT!)

In the end, the PERFECT PIZZA is
a PIZZA SHARED WITH FRIENDS!

STRAWBERRIES

GRAPES

WATERMELLON

CHOCOLATE

PEPPERS

EGGS

BAKED BEAN

PINEAPPLE

FRENCH FRIES

SWEET PEAS

KETCHUP

BACON

OLIVE